One day through a leaf
Is a walk through a town,
From when the sun rises
Until it lies down.

The candle of morning
Is lighted I see,
And catches Giraffe
At his old breakfast tree.

One Day
Scene Through A Leaf

Words & Pictures
by Patrick Dowers

A Star & Elephant Book
from The Green Tiger Press

To Matthew
for help & advice

Text and illustrations copyright ©1981 by
Patrick Dowers
First Edition
First Printing
Paper bound ISBN 0-914676-55-5
Hard bound ISBN 0-914676-56-3
The Green Tiger Press
Box 868
La Jolla, California 92038

Color Separation
by Color Graphics, San Diego, California

This book was set in Souvenir Light,
by Torrey Services, San Diego, California
and
Printed by the Green Tiger Press

While rolling a hoop
By the white picket fence
Surrounding the yard of
The Foote residence,

Let's pause for a drink.
Then onward we'll tread,
Passing the hat house
Of Old Mr. Hedd.

And somewhere in time
An angel was lost;
A heart made of cheesecake
With red icing frost.

The winged giraffe
Near the little cafe
Passed the girl with the birds,
And the dog on its way.

Sit for a trim,
Bounce down the walk,
Or attend to the dodo's
Remarkable talk.

Students are crossing,
They're through for the day.
It's time for a show
Or ballooning away.

The park is a place
To be or to think;
To study giraffes
While they bend for a drink.

To walk by a poolside
Reflecting the sky,
Or chat with a peddlar
With knickknacks to buy.

Leaving the park
At the wood bench we'll stop,
Directly across from
A "Free Turtle" shop.

Where turtles are given
To flaxen haired boys,
And teddybears lunch
By a shop full of toys.

From the window of toyland
We are drawn at last
By a pantalooned hippo
Peddling past.

A star vendor vending;
A message delivered,
A boy with his cats,
And the fishes unrivered.

Past the green mantled houses
We'll ride in our cart,
To the outskirts of town
Our course we will chart.

To the old ivy house
On our walk we will go,
It's next to the home
Of Monsieur Calico.

We're leaving the town
And approaching the sea,
We play for a while
By a house made of tree.

And there's Ted the Toad
Who sits blowing rings.
His mound of a house
Is a lookout for things.

And soon we have come
To the end of our walk,
But pause for a moment
With the Captain to talk.

A turtleback picnic
Departing the reef,
We now say goodbye
To our day through a leaf.